This book is given with love

TO:

_____

FROM:

_____

A Merry Christmas Surprise

The Super Tiny Ghost

Illustrated by:
Catty Flores
David M. E. Virgil

Written by:
Marilee Joy Mayfield

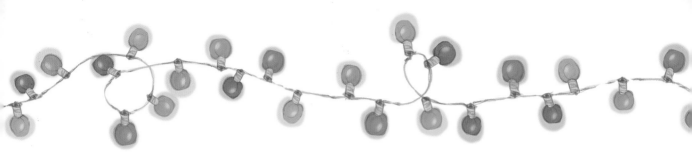

It was cold out at night and there were piles of snow,

But inside the house was a warm Christmas glow.

The super tiny ghost just couldn't wait to see,

How the children had planned to decorate their tree.

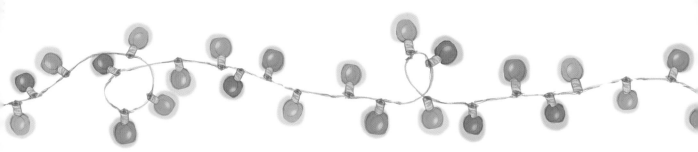

Dad brought down boxes of ornaments one by one,

With piles of tangled lights that needed to be undone.

Mom had made fresh gingerbread for the family to eat,

And hot chocolate with marshmallows for a special treat.

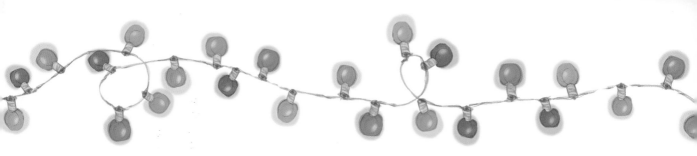

But the super tiny ghost was in a playful mood,
And as the children were enjoying their holiday food,
From the pile of lights, he pulled one bulb aside,
Then flew into the cabinet where he liked to hide.

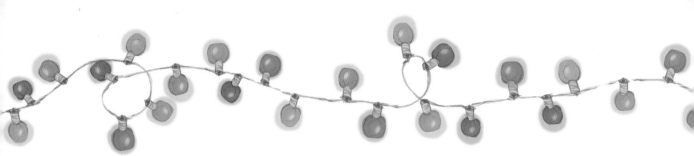

He watched through a hole as Dad adjusted each light.

"That's strange," Dad said. "They're in good and tight...

But nothing seems to happen when I plug the lights in."

Then the super tiny ghost began to sneakily grin.

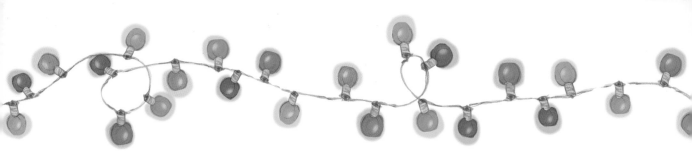

He tried to be quiet...he didn't say a word,

But he let out a giggle that could barely be heard.

The girl gasped, "What's that sound? Did you hear it too?"

The boy nodded, "It must be the ghost! What should we do?"

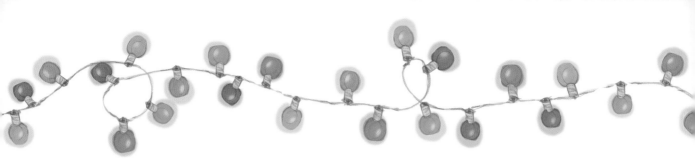

But before they could look for their friend the ghost,

It was time to play holiday hostess and host.

Grandpa and Grandma were knocking at the door,

With gifts that could stack from ceiling to floor.

"Merry Christmas!" said Grandma. "Let me hug the both of you."

"Wow!" said Grandpa. "You've grown since we saw you two."

The boy hugged his grandpa, "We couldn't wait for you to get here!"

The girl piped in, "We've missed you since last year!"

Mom said, "You arrived just in time to help us decorate.

We pulled everything from the attic and started to uncrate."

Grandpa studied the tree. "Don't the lights go on first?"

Dad sighed. "Yeah, these tangled lights are the worst!"

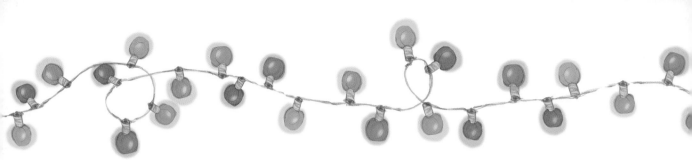

Before more was said, there was a giggling sound.

"What was that?" asked Grandma as she glanced around.

The girl spoke quietly, "Someone else lives with us,

A super tiny ghost who sometimes makes a fuss."

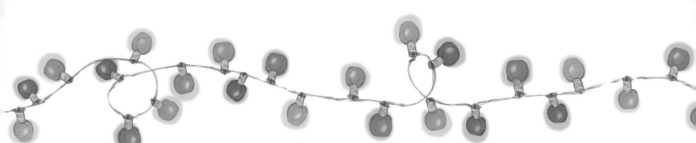

"That's spooky," said Grandpa, "but it's kind of cool too.

What kinds of things does this tiny ghost do?"

The girl smiled. "He's friends with the bats that live in the attic."

The boy nodded. "And causes wooden creaks and electrical static."

"Does he giggle?" asked Grandma. "That's what I thought I heard."

"Yes," said the girl, "Groans and moans too, but never a word."

"Oh, dear!" said Grandma. "I can't sleep in such a noisy house."

"Don't worry," said the boy, "at night, he's as quiet as a mouse."

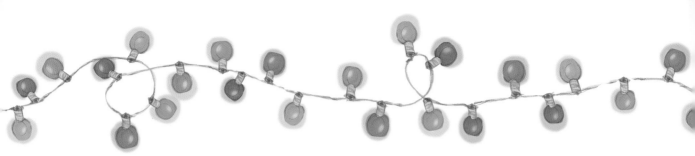

Grandpa stood up. "The giggling came from the cabinet here.

I don't think there's anything inside to fear."

The tiny ghost got nervous and curled up into a ball,

When Grandpa opened the door, he flew out fast down the hall.

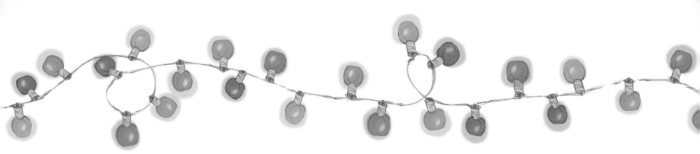

"What was that?!" shrieked Grandma, who turned white as a sheet.

"That's our ghost," said Mom. "I promise, he's super sweet."

"That's odd," said Grandpa. "There's a Christmas light on the shelf."

"Could it be a missing bulb?" said Dad. "I checked the lights myself."

So Grandpa and Dad found the spot for the missing light,

But when the tree turned on, they were met with an odd sight.

The lights flashed in patterns of orange, purple, and green.

They weren't Christmasy at all- they looked like Halloween!

It wasn't only the lights on the tree that were bizarre,

The super tiny ghost had taken his prank quite far.

The tree made sounds like howling winds in a storm,

And it buzzed with low hums like bees in a swarm.

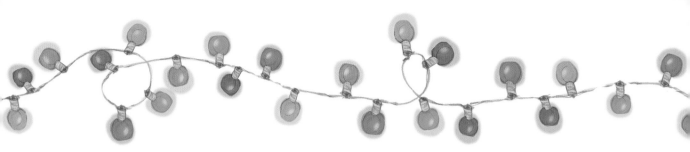

"I think your ghost has made our Christmas tree spooky,"
Said Grandma. "His sense of humor is decidedly kooky."
Then she laughed out loud- it was just so outrageous,
And they all broke into laughter...it was downright contagious.

When the laughing subsided, they all wiped their eyes,
"I know!" said Grandpa. "Let's give your ghost a surprise.
Maybe if we get him a Christmas tree of his own,
He'll stop haunting ours and leave it alone."

The boy cheered. "What a great idea! Let's get it today."
The girl asked, "Can I come along? Can I have a say?"
"Of course," said Mom. "We should all go along.
We know what he likes, so we can't go wrong."

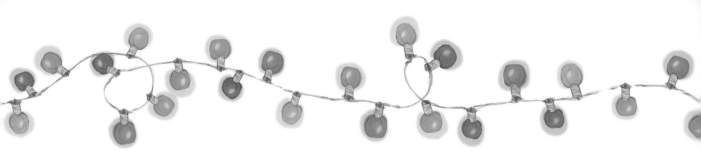

They went to buy a tree, but there weren't many on the lot.

The owner said, "Sorry, this is all that we've got."

Then Grandma found it, it was the perfect ghostly tree...

It was covered with cobwebs and marked, "Take me! I'm free!"

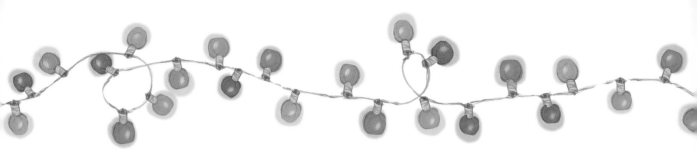

When they got back home, there was quite a surprise,

The whole family just couldn't believe their own eyes!

The ornaments were hung on the tree with great care,

It was almost as if Santa himself had been there!

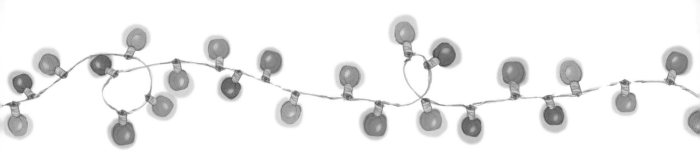

The packages were arranged in an organized pile,

Everything had been done with finesse and style.

The super tiny ghost had decorated the tree.

Even the Christmas lights now worked perfectly.

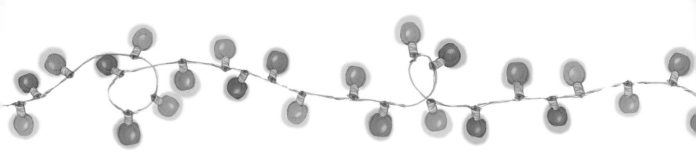

"Amazing!" said Grandma. "Your ghost should come visit me."

"Incredible!" smiled Mom. "This is our best Christmas tree!"

"Awesome!" cheered the boy and girl at the same exact time.

Dad added, "Look! The bells even sway as they chime!"

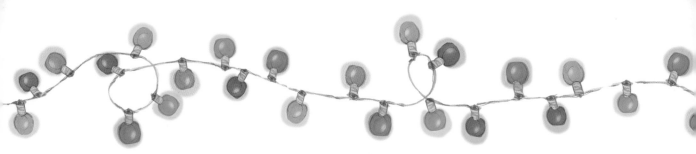

They took his tree to the basement, the ghost's favorite place,

It was a strange little tree, with no beauty or grace.

But the super tiny ghost loved having something green—

He decorated it with things that reminded him of Halloween.

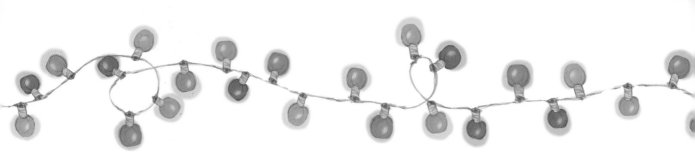

The fireplace was roaring, and his family was upstairs,

They were laughing and happy and free of daily cares.

It was the Merriest Christmas in his home by the sea,

And for the super tiny ghost it was the perfect place to be.

🐾 Claim Your FREE Gift!

Visit ➡ PDICBooks.com/STGChristmas

Thank you for purchasing The Super Tiny Ghost: A Merry Christmas Surprise, and welcome to the Puppy Dogs & Ice Cream family.

We're certain you're going to love the little gift we've prepared for you at the website above.